Sunny
63

This book is dedicated to all friends of nature—
young, old, human, or kappa.

ABOUT TUTTLE
"Books to Span the East and West"

Our core mission at Tuttle Publishing is to create books which bring people together one page at a time. Tuttle was founded in 1832 in the small New England town of Rutland, Vermont (USA). Our fundamental values remain as strong today as they were then—to publish best-in-class books informing the English-speaking world about the countries and peoples of Asia. The world has become a smaller place today and Asia's economic, cultural and political influence has expanded, yet the need for meaningful dialogue and information about this diverse region has never been greater. Since 1948, Tuttle has been a leader in publishing books on the cultures, arts, cuisines, languages and literatures of Asia. Our authors and photographers have won numerous awards and Tuttle has published thousands of books on subjects ranging from martial arts to paper crafts. We welcome you to explore the wealth of information available on Asia at www.tuttlepublishing.com.

Published by Tuttle Publishing, an imprint of Periplus Editions (HK) Ltd.

www.tuttlepublishing.com

Bilingual Edition Copyright © 2016 by Sunny Seki.

Library of Congress Cataloging in Process

ISBN 978-4-8053- 1399-2
(Previously published as ISBN 978-4-8053-1088-5)

Distributed by

North America, Latin America & Europe
Tuttle Publishing
364 Innovation Drive
North Clarendon, VT
05759-9436 U.S.A.
Tel: 1 (802) 773-8930; Fax: 1 (802) 773-6993
info@tuttlepublishing.com
www.tuttlepublishing.com

Japan
Tuttle Publishing
Yaekari Building, 3rd Floor
5-4-12 Osaki
Shinagawa-ku
Tokyo 141 0032
Tel: (81) 3 5437-0171; Fax: (81) 3 5437-0755
sales@tuttle.co.jp
www.tuttle.co.jp

Asia Pacific
Berkeley Books Pte. Ltd.
61 Tai Seng Avenue #02-12
Singapore 534167
Tel: (65) 6280-1330; Fax: (65) 6280-6290
inquiries@periplus.com.sg
www.periplus.com

First edition
20 19 18 17 16   10 9 8 7 6 5 4 3 2 1

Printed in Hong Kong   1606EP

Who will take care of the water?

THE LAST KAPPA OF OLD JAPAN

A MAGICAL JOURNEY OF TWO FRIENDS

BILINGUAL **ENGLISH** AND **JAPANESE** EDITION

日本最後のカッパ

Story and illustrations by
SUNNY SEKI

文と絵・サニー関

TUTTLE Publishing

Tokyo │ Rutland, Vermont │ Singapore

Our story begins in Old Japan, just before the time of electricity. In the peaceful countryside, a green land with clean, clear streams, there lived a boy named Norihei. His family had been farmers for many generations.

むかしむかし、日本に電灯がつく前のお話です。
大自然と、きれいな水があふれる田舎に、
のり平という男の子が住ん
でいました。
先祖はみんな
農家です。

Norihei grew up eating fresh food with neighbors who shared their fruits and vegetables. But he didn't just eat the food; he had to cook and clean up too! He even learned to serve each dish correctly, because in Old Japan it was the custom for children to serve their elders.

のり平の村では、お隣りと野菜や魚を交換します。食事は食べるだけでなく、料理や片づけも大切。子供は給仕をしたりして、お皿の並べ方や作法を学びます。

Norihei knew that plants need good soil, sunshine, and water. He was proud that his cucumbers were growing especially big.

農業には良い土、日光、たくさんの水が必要です。のり平が注意深く育てた今年のキュウリは豊作です。

One day while working in his garden, Norihei heard a loud moan, and was amazed to see a strange creature with webbed hands and spots on his back. Norihei had never seen one, but he was sure ... this must be a kappa!

ある日、畑でウーンと苦しそうな声が聞こえたので駆けよると、手と足に水かき、背中に斑点のある子供が倒れているではありませんか！のり平は、はじめてでしたが、「こりゃあ、カッパみたいだ」と思いました。

"Are you okay?" Norihei asked the creature.

"I've been out of the water too long because I've been eating your tasty cucumbers. Now I'm too weak to go home!" the creature replied in a tiny voice.

"Wow!" thought Norihei. "It really is a kappa!"

「君、大丈夫？」と声をかけると、「ここのキュウリはおいしくて、食べていたら体が乾いちゃった。水がないと死んじゃうよ〜」と、か弱く答えます。

「キュウリが大好物のカッパって、やっぱり　いたんだなぁ」と、のり平は出会いにビックリ。

Norihei splashed water on the kappa, who quickly grew strong again.

"Oh, thank you. You are very kind. I will be forever grateful to you for saving my life!"

Norihei had heard that kappas were troublemakers, but he liked this one. So he gave him some cucumbers to take home.

水をかけてあげると、その子は元気になって、「ワァ～、助かった。お礼は必ずするよ。君は優しいね」と大喜び。カッパは乱暴だと聞いていた
のり平は、いじらしくなって、
おみやげにキュウリをあ
げました。

One day while Norihei was fishing, the kappa came swimming up to him.

"I was wondering … what's your name?" the kappa asked.

"I'm Norihei," the boy replied.

The kappa smiled and said, "I'm Kyu. Follow me, and I'll show you where to catch the biggest fish!"

しばらくして、川で魚を釣っていると、いつかのカッパが出てきて「ねぇ、君は何っていう名前なの？」と聞きます。「ぼくは、のり平って言うんだ」と答えると、カッパは「ぼくの名前はQ。ついておいでよ。大きな魚がいるところを教えてあげるから」と誘いました。

Kyu taught Norihei a new way to swim, and Norihei showed
Kyu how to sumo wrestle. They quickly became good friends
and gave each other nicknames – "Kyu-chan" and "Nori-bo."

Qはのり平に泳ぎ方、のり平はQに相撲を教えたりして、お互いを
"Qちゃん""のり坊"と呼び合うほど仲良くなったのです。

"Nori-bo! Be careful! That eel will give you a shock if you touch it!"

Norihei was fascinated as Kyu-chan showed him the secret wonders of the water world.

「のり坊！危ないよ！電気ウナギは触るとショックがくるよ！」Qは水の中の神秘な世界を案内してくれるので、のり平はゴキゲンです。

The two friends often met to play in deep, watery canyons. But not far away, a railroad was being built. Japan was changing quickly.

ふたりは　よく峡谷へ遊びに行きました。しかし、こんな山奥にも鉄道が入り込んで来たのです。だんだん自然環境も変わり出しました。

One afternoon two railroad workers saw Kyu-chan and
Norihei skipping stones. They whispered slyly, "We should
catch that kappa! We can sell it to the aquarium … or maybe
the circus!"

ある日、二人の線路工夫が '飛び石遊び' をしているQと、のり
平を見つけました。そして、ずるがしこく「あのカッパを捕まえ
よう。水族館かサーカスなら高く買ってくれるぞ！」と、ささや
きあったのです。

Norihei saw them coming. "Run, Kyu-chan! They're trying to catch you!"

"Don't worry, Nori-bo! When I reach water, I can use magic to escape!"

"Hurry! There is a well right over there!" Norihei said.

Kyu-chan was puzzled. "Why are they trying to catch me? I didn't do anything wrong!"

最初にのり平が、怪しい二人が駆けてくるのに気づいて、「Ｑちゃん、逃げろ！ねらわれているぞっ！」と叫びました。「大丈夫！ぼくは水さえあれば、消えちゃうことができるから！」と、水桶に駆け寄りましたが、中はカラッポ。「急がなくっちゃ！井戸はあっちだ！」のり平は気が気ではありません。「どうして捕まえるの？ぼくは悪いことしていないのに〜！」Ｑは泣きそうな声を出しています。

Just in time, Kyu-chan jumped head first
into the well. SPLASH! The men peered
inside, but all they saw were ripples.
"We missed him! He got away!"

　もう少しで捕まりそうになった時、Qは
ピョーンと頭から井戸に飛び込んだのです。
「バシャーン！」」水音と同時に、工夫達
は中を覗き込みました。けれども、波紋の
ほかに何も見えません。「しまった。逃げら
れた！」

A few days later Kyu-chan told Norihei some sad news.

"Nori-bo, my family says we have to move. Our job is to keep the water clean, but this area is getting dangerous. My parents are worried. But before I go I want to give you this crystal necklace. It's shaped like a water drop. If you ever need help with water, drop this into a stream and call me."

After that day, Norihei would not see his friend for a very long time.

数日後、Ｑはのり平に悲しい知らせを伝えました。「うちの家族は引越しするんだって。カッパの仕事は水をきれいにすることだけど、このあたりは危なくなってきた。ぼくの両親は最近、仕事が増えて大変だと言っている。それでネ、お別れに君に水晶の首飾りをあげるよ。これは水玉の形なんだ。もし、いつか水に関して助けが必要なときは、水に投げ込んでぼくを呼んでくれれば良い」

そうやって二人の友達は別れたまま、長い年月が経ったのです。

Twenty years passed, and the once peaceful countryside
was now a busy town with electricity and big factories.

二十年が過ぎ、田舎はにぎやかになり、電気がきて
工場が建ちはじめました。

Norihei was no longer a boy, but a grown man. He had a wife named Hana, a baby girl named Kaya, and a dog named Maru. Norihei still lived in the same house. But the front part was now a restaurant.

のり平もすっかり大人になりました。彼の家族は、妻のはな、娘のかや、そして犬のマルです。のり平は家を直して、食堂をはじめました。

Norihei's restaurant was very busy. He was a good chef, and people liked his fresh new recipes. And Hana was a hard-working manager.

のり平食堂は、とても繁盛していました。のり平の料理は、新鮮でおいしいと大評判です。妻のはなも一緒に働いています。

One day, while Norihei and Hana were very busy, baby Kaya ran outside to chase a butterfly. Only Maru the dog saw what happened.

ある日、二人が忙しい最中、娘のかやはちょうちょを追っていました。
そして、犬のマルだけが、何が起こったのかを見ていたのです。

"Arff-arff!" Maru barked. Norihei and Hana ran outside. Kaya's pinwheel was on the ground, but Kaya was gone. It seemed that she had fallen into the stream.

「ワンワン♪」マルが、あまりに吠えるので、のり平とはなは、何事かと外へ出てみました。すると、かやの風車が下水の近くに落ちていて、彼女がいません。それを見て、かやは水に落ちたと両親にはピンときたのです。

Norihei and Hana ran frantically through the streets, asking everyone if they had seen a baby.

驚いたのり平とはなは、かやを見た人はいないかと叫びながら、夢中で川沿いを駆け出しました。のり平はこんなに早く走ったことはなかったので、ついにくたびれてしまいました。

Hours passed, evening came, but the search crew had found nothing.

"We're very sorry," they apologized, "but we can't work in the dark. We'll have to wait until morning."

Norihei gazed into the water. He had never felt so sad in all his life. Then suddenly he remembered the necklace his old friend had given him.

夕暮れになっても救助隊員は何も発見できず、「残念ですが、暗くなったので明日の朝捜し直します」と、伝えにきました。

のり平は、じっと、さびしく水面を見つめたまま言葉もありません。

と、突然、むかしカッパにもらった首飾りを思い出したのです。

"This is my last hope. Kyu-chan ... please ... if you're still out there, find our baby!"

Norihei took a deep breath and dropped the necklace into the water. Hana looked puzzled. Norihei told her about the kappa, and about the necklace and the promise that came with it. But Hana's face was still full of doubt and despair.

「もう、これしかない。Ｑちゃん、お願いだ。水に落ちた娘を助けてくれ、頼む！」

そう言って、のり平は深く息を吸うと、首飾りを水に投げ込みました。はなが、不思議そうな顔をしているので、のり平は旧友のカッパとの約束を話して聞かせました。しかし、彼女の青ざめた顔から疑いと不安は消えません。

It was after midnight, but Norihei and Hana couldn't sleep. The only sounds they heard were the ticking of the clock and the howling of the wind. They were beginning to lose hope.

真夜中を過ぎても眠れないまま、のり平とはなは、希望を失いかけていました。
聞こえるのは、柱時計と風の音ばかり。

Suddenly, Maru leaped up and barked. Someone was knocking at the door.
Norihei and Hana looked at each other.

  "Who could it be?"

その時です。マルが急に飛び起き、激しく吠え始めたのです。続いて誰かが戸
を叩く音。のり平とはなは、顔を見合わせました。
  「今頃、誰が来たんだろうか？」

"Kyu-chan! … Is that really you?" Norihei shouted.

It was the kappa. He was much older, and he was carrying a baby. "My baby!" cried Hana. She and Norihei were overjoyed.

"Sorry for the delay," Kyu-chan said as he stumbled in. "I had to come at night so I wouldn't be seen. I searched everywhere to find your daughter, and I kept my promise!"

戸口には、年とったカッパが、女の子を背負い立っていました。「Qちゃん！Qちゃんだよね？」のり平は、夢かと疑いました。「かやちゃん！」と、はなの叫び声。無事な娘を見て、夫婦の顔は喜びでクシャクシャです。「遅くなってすまん。誰かに見つかるとまずいんで、夜中に訪ねることにした。いやぁ、娘さんを捜すのは大変だったが、約束を守れて良かった」しわがれた声でそう言うと、Qはよろけながら土間に入ってきました。

"Thank you!" said Norihei.

The two friends hugged, crying tears of joy.

"How have you been, Nori-bo?"

"I'm fine, Kyu-chan. But you have some cuts and bruises! Let me clean them for you."

「ありがとう！」のり平は、ほかに何を言っていいのかわからず、二人は、うれし涙で抱き合いました。「久しぶりだねぇ～　のり坊。元気かい？」「あぁ、元気だとも。Qちゃん。ところで、さっき気がついたけど、君の体は切り傷だらけだ。まず、手当てをさせてくれ」

Norihei said, "When you first came in, I thought I was seeing your father!"

"Yes, I do look a lot older … That happens to kappas when the environment is not right. The rest of my family have all died. I'm the last kappa alive."

Norihei remembered that the kappa's job is to keep the water clean. "If you die, who will take care of the water?"

Kyu-chan looked serious. "It will have to be you humans."

「最初、ぼくはQちゃんのお父さんが来たかと思ったよ！」

「ウン、無理もない。われわれカッパは住みにくくなると、早く年を取る。うちの一家はみんな死んで、生きているのは、ぼくだけになってしまった」

それを聞いてのり平は、カッパは水をきれいにするのが仕事だったと思い出し、質問したのです。「それじゃ、もし君が死んだら誰が水をきれいにするんだい？」

Qは少し困った顔で、「そうなったら人間しかいない。君たちの番だ！」と答えました。

Norihei wanted
to give Kyu-chan
a special treat. Suddenly
he had an idea. "Kyu-chan,
because it's your favorite food,
I've created a special sushi roll made
with … cucumbers! I'll call it the Kappa Roll!"
　Kyu-chan was very excited. "Wow, I can't wait to try it!"

のり平は、Qに何かお礼をしたくなりました。と、ひらめいたものがあります。
　「Qちゃん、特製の巻き寿司を食べていってくれよ、中に好物のキュウリを入れるからさ。そうだ、"カッパ巻き"と名づけよう！」
　「うわぁ、そりゃ、待ちどおしいネ」Qは大喜び。

"That was delicious, but now I have to go back to work."

"Good-bye, Kyu-chan! I'm lucky to have a friend like you!" said Norihei.

Hana packed some Kappa Rolls in a box, and said, "Take this with you. We want you to live for centuries!"

Kyu-chan replied, "And I want you to keep making Kappa Rolls for centuries too!" Everyone laughed as they waved goodbye.

From that day, the Kappa Roll became a popular dish at Norihei's restaurant. And today it is enjoyed throughout Japan. But most people don't realize that inside every Kappa Roll is wrapped the friendship of two special friends who chose to save each other.

「あ〜、おいしかった。ごちそうさま。さ、仕事にもどらなくっちゃ」

「元気でね、Qちゃん。君のような友だちがいて、ぼくは幸せだよ！」と、のり平は感謝しました。はなは、カッパ巻きを箱に入れ、「持ち帰って食べて下さい。あなたには、あと何世紀も長生きをしてもらいたいですから…」と、渡すと、Qは「ぼくも君たちに、あと何世紀も生きてカッパ巻きを作って下さいって、言おうと思ってたんだ」と、茶目っ気たっぷりに答えてみんなで大笑い。「さようなら」と言いあいながら、Qは川の方へ遠ざかっていきました。

やがて、カッパ巻きは、のり平食堂の人気メニューとなりました。今では日本中で好まれていますが、ほとんどの人はカッパ巻きに、命を救いあった二人の友情が包み込まれているとは知らず、パクついているのです。

CULTURAL NOTES

❀ The kappa, translated "river child," has been a part of Japanese folklore for hundreds of years. Believed to be messengers of the god of water, kappas have their own shrines. They appear as statues or signs in rivers, swamps, and lakes, and they often become the name of a bridge or other landmark.

❀ Japanese waters are full of creatures, including dangerous salamanders, turtles, frogs, and other amphibians, and it is commonly believed that kappa images evolved from the features of these animals. These typically include a beak, turtle back, webbed limbs, greenish skin, and a shaved head that can hold water. Many of these kappa images and related stories were scary, so they became part of the vast folklore of Japanese *yokai* (frightening monsters with mysterious powers). There were no lifeguards in old Japan, so parents often told their children about kappas to prevent them from venturing too close to the water.

❀ Kappas are mischievous, and they like to eat Japanese cucumbers. When they were introduced to America, they took on another form called Ninja Turtles, and started eating pizza instead of cucumbers!

❀ *Kappamaki*, or kappa rolls, are a popular type of sushi roll made of thinly-sliced cucumbers and rice wrapped in *nori* (dried seaweed).

❀ Japan has four distinct seasons, which are richly reflected in its heritage and art. Rice planting occurs in late spring, and harvest takes place in early autumn. Japan is a small country, so farmers learned to maximize their planting area by creating terraced hillsides called *dan-dan batake*.

❀ The illustrations in this story show how Japanese houses evolved. First came the *noka*—a traditional straw-roofed farmhouse, with the upstairs area designed for raising silkworms. As cities developed, the straw roofs became tile, and houses were attached to each other.

❀ Japan had closed its doors to foreign influence until 1868, the beginning of the era of Emperor Meiji. Now Japan joined the West in the Industrial Revolution, modernizing the entire country. Changes happened quickly—from factories and railroads, to even fashion and hairstyles. These are seen throughout this story, with a clear contrast depicted between the setting on pages 2–3 and the setting on pages 16–17.